Naomi Knows
It's Springtime

by Virginia L. Kroll

illustrated by Jill Kastner

CAROLINE HOUSE
BOYDS MILLS PRESS

Text copyright © 1993
by Virginia L. Kroll
Illustrations copyright © 1993
by Jill Kastner

Published by Caroline House
Boyds Mills Press, Inc.
A Highlights Company
910 Church Street
Honesdale, Pennsylvania 18431

Publisher Cataloging-in-Publication Data
Kroll, Virginia L.
    Naomi knows it's springtime / by
Virginia L. Kroll ; illustrated by Jill
Kastner. —1st ed.
[32]p. : col. ill. ; cm.
Summary: A young blind girl experi-
ences the first signs of spring.
ISBN 1-56397-006-6
1. Spring—Juvenile fiction.
2. Blindness—Juvenile fiction.
(1. Spring—Fiction. 2. Blind—Fiction.)
I. Kastner, Jill, ill. II. Title.
   (F)—dc20   1993
Library of Congress Catalog Card
Number: 92-71267

First edition, 1993
Book designed by Tim Gillner
The text of this book is set in
12-point Americana.
The illustrations are oil paintings.
Distributed by St. Martin's Press
Printed in the United States of America
Hong Kong

10 9 8 7 6 5 4 3 2 1

For my daughter,
Katya Haeick
          —V.L.K.

For Nancy Carpenter
          —J.K.

Naomi knows it's springtime when the air stops nipping her nose and chin

and kisses her cheeks instead.

Naomi knows it's springtime when the gutters overflow with rushing rain

and aren't bent and cracked and stiffened with frosted ice.

She knows it's spring when she hears the squeaks of newborn nestlings

instead of the chilling squeals of autumn's stragglers left behind.

Naomi knows it's springtime when wind whispers secrets to the trees

and doesn't screech and bellow at the houses anymore. 11

Naomi knows it's spring when she's warm in bed with her quilt cast aside

and her feet don't curl against the cold bathroom tiles.

13

Naomi knows it's springtime when her swing holds her in a safe, round hug

and she sails and spins in a whirling twirl.

She knows it's springtime when lilies and lilacs perfume the yard

and lawn mower motors vibrate in her ears.

Naomi knows it's springtime when a fluttering ladybug lands

and gently tickles her unmittened hand.

When friends call "Naomi" through the screen

instead of ringing the doorbell chime, Naomi knows it's springtime.

Naomi knows it's springtime when cool grass blades slide between her toes

and warm sand grains trickle through her groping fingers.

Naomi knows it's springtime when

the sweetness of chocolate custard runs over her tingling tongue. 25

Naomi knows it's springtime when her golden dog Damsel rolls in the grass

instead of shivering in the snow.

27

Naomi knows it's springtime when Mrs. Jensen next door sighs,

"If only Naomi could see the blue in the sky!"

Then Naomi smiles and says,

"If only Mrs. Jensen could see the rainbow in my mind!"